KT-199-687

MISSING!

Flame

Have you seen this kitten?

Flame is a magic kitten of royal blood, missing from his own world.
His uncle, Ebony, is very keen that he is found quickly.
Flame may be hard to spot as he often appears in a
variety of fluffy kitten colours but you can recognize him
by his big emerald eyes and whiskers that crackle with magic!

He is believed to be looking for a young friend to take care of him.

Could it be you?

If you find this very special kitten please let Ebony,
ruler of the Lion Throne, know.

Sue Bentley's books for children often include animals or fairies. She lives in Northampton and enjoys reading, going to the cinema, and sitting watching the frogs and newts in her garden pond. If she hadn't been a writer, she would probably have been a skydiver or a brain surgeon. The main reason she writes is that she can drink pots and pots of tea while she's typing. She has met and owned many cats and each one has brought a special sort of magic to her life.

Magic Kitten

Classroom Chaos

SUE BENTLEY

Illustrated by Angela Swan

PUFFIN

Brian – the shy blue twin

PUFFIN BOOKS

Published by the Penguin Group
Penguin Books Ltd, 80 Strand, London WC2R 0RL, England
Penguin Group (USA) Inc., 375 Hudson Street, New York, New York 10014, USA
Penguin Group (Canada), 90 Eglinton Avenue East, Suite 700, Toronto, Ontario,
Canada M4P 2Y3 (a division of Pearson Penguin Canada Inc.)
Penguin Ireland, 25 St Stephen's Green, Dublin 2, Ireland (a division
of Penguin Books Ltd)
Penguin Group (Australia), 250 Camberwell Road, Camberwell, Victoria 3124, Australia
(a division of Pearson Australia Group Pty Ltd)
Penguin Books India Pvt Ltd, 11 Community Centre, Panchsheel Park,
New Delhi – 110 017, India
Penguin Group (NZ), cnr Airborne and Rosedale Roads, Albany, Auckland 1310,
New Zealand (a division of Pearson New Zealand Ltd)
Penguin Books (South Africa) (Pty) Ltd, 24 Sturdee Avenue, Rosebank,
Johannesburg 2196, South Africa

Penguin Books Ltd, Registered Offices: 80 Strand, London WC2R 0RL, England

penguin.com

First published 2006
6

Text copyright © Susan Bentley, 2006
Illustrations copyright © Angela Swan, 2006
All rights reserved

The moral right of the author and illustrator has been asserted

Set in Bembo by Palimpsest Book Production Limited,
Polmont, Stirlingshire
Made and printed in England by Clays Ltd, St Ives plc

British Library Cataloguing in Publication Data
A CIP catalogue record for this book is available from the British Library

ISBN-13: 978–0–141–32015–1
ISBN-10: 0–141–32015–X

Prologue

'Disguise yourself, Prince Flame! It isn't
safe for you to be back here. Your
uncle is close by!' Cirrus urged the
young white lion who stood beside
him in the cave behind the waterfall.

Flame's fur crackled with silver
sparks. There was a dazzling white flash
and there, in his place, now stood a
tiny, fluffy, black and white kitten.

Cirrus leaned down and brushed his old grey muzzle against the top of the kitten's fluffy head. 'You must go back to the other world, Prince Flame. But stay in this disguise. It will serve you well.'

Suddenly a menacing growl split the air.

Flame looked up at Cirrus, his emerald eyes flashing. 'Uncle Ebony rules my kingdom. One day I will return and claim my throne!' he mewed bravely.

Cirrus's worn teeth flashed in a brief smile. 'Yes, you will, my prince. But only once your powers have become stronger. Go now! Hide!'

Just as Flame scrambled behind a rock, an enormous adult lion burst

through the curtain of water. His huge
paws thudded on the wet rock.

'Cirrus! Tell me where my nephew is
hiding!' Ebony demanded.

Behind the rock, Flame's tiny body
trembled in fear.

Cirrus growled. 'Prince Flame is far
away. You will never find him!'

Ebony roared with rage. 'My spies are
looking for him. Flame cannot hide
from me forever . . .'

Behind the rock, Flame felt the
power building inside him. He let out a
tiny miaow as silver sparks ignited in
his black and white fur. The cave began
to fade, and he felt himself falling.
Falling . . .

Chapter
* ONE *

'Bye! See you at the end of term!' Abi
West called to her parents from the
upstairs window.

As the car pulled away out of
Brockinghurst School's car park, Abi
turned back to her new room. She felt
excited but a bit nervous. It was going
to seem strange to share with someone
she didn't know.

'Might as well unpack,' she decided,
lifting her case on to one of the beds.

There were two single beds with blue
quilts and bedside cupboards. Blue
checked curtains and a red rug made
the room bright and cosy.

From the window, she saw that more
cars were pulling into the front drive.
Girls in uniform were getting out and
saying goodbye to their families.

Abi had just finished piling away her clothes and books when the door crashed open with a bang.

A pretty fair-haired girl marched into the room. She scowled at Abi. 'Who are you?'

'Hi,' Abi said. 'I'm Abi West.'

'Well, you're in my room,' the girl said rudely.

'I thought I could choose any room,' Abi said. 'I've just put all my stuff away.'

The other girl put her hands on her hips. 'And I'm supposed to care? You'll just have to move it, won't you?'

Abi blinked at her, unsure what to do. The other girl looked about eleven, a year older than Abi.

'I thought it was your voice I could

hear, Keera Moore,' said a calm voice
from the doorway.

Abi spun round. She saw a tall
woman with a pleasant face. It was Mrs
York, the head teacher. There was a
small, slim girl with her.

Keera changed completely. 'Oh, hello,
Mrs York,' she said with a smile. 'Abi
here was just saying she didn't mind
moving to another room.'

'No, I wasn't!' Abi said indignantly.
'You told me this was your room. And
that I had to move out!'

Keera glared at her, blue eyes flashing.
'You little sneak,' she hissed.

'That's enough, Keera,' the Head said.
'You know very well that rooms are
never reserved at Brockinghurst.' She
turned to Abi. 'Abi West, I want you to

meet Sasha Parekh. I thought it might be a good idea for you two to share this term. You'll both have a lot in common. It's the first time either of you has been away from home.'

'Ah, diddums,' Keera sneered under her breath.

Abi smiled at Sasha, who was very pretty with dark eyes and olive skin. She wore her thick black hair in a long plait. On one cheek she had a red birthmark.

'It's really nice to meet you,' Abi said. Sasha seemed a hundred times nicer that Keera already!

'You too,' Sasha said shyly.

'I've got some animal posters to put on the wall. Would you like to help me?' Abi asked.

Sasha dark eyes lit up. 'Definitely! I love animals.'

'So do I. Especially big cats,' Abi said, warming to Sasha.

Keera pointed a finger at her open mouth and made pretend gagging sounds.

Mrs York frowned at her. 'This room seems to be taken, Keera. I suggest you try the one next door. It's identical to this one.'

'Oh, all right.' Keera rolled her eyes
as she stomped outside with her case.
Mrs York turned back to Abi and
Sasha. 'I'll leave you two to settle in.
Come down to the hall when you hear
the bell. You'll meet your teachers and
collect your lesson timetables.'

'She's nice, isn't she?' Abi said to
Sasha after the Head had left.

Sasha nodded.

Suddenly a lot of banging came from
the room next door. Then a voice
complained, 'This is a grotty room!
And this school is a smelly dump! I
hate being back here!'

Sasha looked at Abi. 'Keera!' they
chorused. The two of them fell about
laughing.

★

'Phew! There's so much to remember,' groaned Abi. She sat down beside Sasha at a table in the main hall.

The room had wooden beams and walls of dark, carved wood. An enormous fireplace took up most of the end wall. The room was buzzing with girls and teachers, and everyone seemed to be talking at once.

Sasha bit her nails nervously. 'I can't remember any of the teachers' names or where the classrooms are.'

'Nor me. But I expect we'll soon get used to it,' Abi said.

'Well! If it isn't the sneak,' a voice behind her said.

Abi didn't need to turn round to know who it was. 'Hello, Keera,' she said.

Keera came up and leaned her
elbows on the table. She was with two
other girls. One had brown hair and
freckles and the other was tall and slim
with black curly hair.

Abi remembered hearing their names
called out earlier that day: Marsha
Clarke and Tiwa Rhames.

'Have you brought your teddies to
help you sleep?' Keera said in a
mocking, baby voice.

Tiwa sniggered. 'After all, we
wouldn't want you to have nightmares
about the ghost.'

'What ghost?' asked Abi. 'You're
making it up. There's no such thing.'

Keera smirked. 'Oh, no? Haven't you
heard about the Grey Lady of
Brockinghurst? She haunts the school's

corridors, lying in wait for snotty little first years. I'd watch out if I were you!' She turned to Marsha and Tiwa. 'Come on, let's go and see if the tuck shop's open.'

The girls nudged each other and laughed as they walked away.

Sasha glanced nervously at Abi. 'Do you think there really is a ghost?' she asked. 'Most old buildings are supposed to be haunted, aren't they?'

Abi smiled at her as she gathered up all the pages she'd been given. 'Keera was just trying to scare us. Don't look so worried.' She turned to her school bag. 'Oh, I've forgotten the folder for our next class. I think I'll just dash upstairs and get it.'

'OK. I'll wait here,' Sasha said,

looking more relaxed now.

Abi found the nearest doorway and went out of the hall. Hurrying past a row of classrooms, she found a narrow stairway leading upwards. Five minutes later, after countless twists and turns, Abi stopped on a gloomy landing.

'Oh, great! I'm totally lost,' she said aloud.

Abi looked around. Narrow windows of thick glass were set into the walls. Dust swirled in the shafts of light that managed to get through. In front of her there was an ancient door, covered with cobwebs. She pushed at it with her fingertips. It slowly creaked open.

She looked into the gloom, where dark shapes were visible. As her eyes adjusted to the dimness, she saw stacks of old furniture. It was just an old storeroom.

Then suddenly Abi caught something out of the corner of her eye – something pale and glowing. She gasped. It must be the Grey Lady!

Frozen to the spot, Abi gradually began to realize the glow wasn't actually human-shaped at all. But what could it be?

She crept closer into the storeroom. Something was lying across two whole chairs. Abi frowned – it looked like a sparkly furry blanket. As she took another step there came a low rumbling purr.

Abi blinked in disbelief. The 'blanket' looked like a young white lion! He was fast asleep.

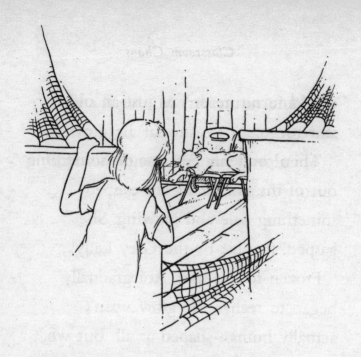

She stared at the silver sparkles
gleaming in the lion's fur. He looked
fierce but beautiful. Abi's heart beat
fast. She didn't know whether to stay
or run away.

'How did a *lion* get here?' she whispered to herself.

The white lion's eyes flew open. He
lifted into a crouch. The hair along his
back stood up in a spiked ridge.

'Come no nearer! My teeth are sharp and my claws are strong!' he growled.

Abi almost jumped out of her skin in terror. 'You can talk!' she gasped.

Chapter
TWO

For a moment the lion just stared at
Abi with its piercing emerald eyes.

Abi sensed that it was more
frightened than angry. She crouched
down to make herself seem smaller.
'It's OK. I won't hurt you,' she said
softly.

The lion relaxed and pricked up its
ears. 'I do not mean to scare you. I

thought you were an enemy,' he said in
a deep, velvety growl.

'What . . .? Who are you?' Abi
stammered.

'Flame.' The lion dipped his head in
greeting. 'Prince Flame. Heir to the
Lion Throne,' he told her solemnly.

Abi dipped her head in return. It
seemed the right thing to do. 'Where
are you from?'

'Far away,' Flame replied with a sad
look in his eyes.

Abi began to recover from her fear of
Flame. She took a step forward and
stretched her hand out. 'I'm Abi. This
is my first term at boarding school. Is it
OK if I touch you . . .?'

'Wait! Stay back!' Flame ordered.

There was a silver flash.

'Oh!' Blinded, Abi put her hands over her eyes. When she looked again, she saw that the white lion had gone. In his place stood a fluffy, black and white kitten with emerald-green eyes.

'Where's Flame?' Abi gasped.

'I am Flame,' the kitten mewed in a tiny voice. 'This is my disguise. I am in hiding. My Uncle Ebony is trying to find me. To kill me.'

'But why would your uncle want to kill you?' Abi asked.

'To steal my throne. To keep it. Can you help me, Abi?'

'Of course I will!' She leaned forward and picked up the kitten. 'You can live in my room. Just wait until Sasha sees you!'

Flame wriggled. He reached up a tiny paw and touched her chin. 'No! You can tell no one. It must be our secret,' he urged.

Abi frowned. She felt sure that Sasha could keep a secret.

'You must promise,' Flame insisted. He blinked up at her with wide, trusting eyes.

Abi felt her heart turn over. She didn't want to do anything that put him in danger. 'OK, I promise,' she agreed.

Then she had a sudden thought. Pupils weren't allowed pets. How was she going to sneak Flame into her room?

Abi tucked Flame beneath her sweater. 'Sorry. I have to do this,' she said as the kitten looked up at her indignantly. 'Don't wriggle now, OK?'

Luckily, most of the school were still in the hall. She managed to find her way back to her room without being seen.

'Here we are,' she whispered, putting Flame on her bed.

Flame's eyes scanned the room and then he gave a whiskery grin. 'A safe place,' he mewed, pointing a black and white paw at the wardrobe.

'You want to go up there?' It was a good idea, Abi thought. If he slept at the back against the wall, he'd be out of sight of anyone unless they stood on the bed. 'OK. I'll find something soft to make you a cosy nest.'

As Abi began searching in a drawer, Flame's ears pricked. He gave an urgent little miaow. 'Abi! Someone is coming.'

'Oh, no!' Abi whipped round.
She saw the door handle turning.
There wasn't enough time to hide
Flame!

Suddenly Abi felt a strange, tingly
feeling down her spine. Silver sparkles
leapt from Flame's fur and his whiskers
crackled. Little points of light popped
in the air around him.

Something very strange was
happening.

Keera stuck her head round the door.
'I thought I heard voices in here.' She
looked straight at the bed where Flame
sat!

Abi's breath caught in her throat.
Keera would tell the Head about
Flame! Before she could say anything,
Keera spoke up.

24

'I thought so!' Keera's mouth twisted
in a triumphant grin. 'There's no one
else in here! You're such a big baby,
Abi West. Wait until I tell everyone
that I caught you talking to your
imaginary friend!'

Abi looked back at the bed in
confusion. Flame sat there large as life,
but Keera couldn't see him!

She turned back to Keera. 'Tell them

what you like! See if I care,' she
said.

Keera looked disappointed. She
turned on her toes and slammed the
bedroom door in a huff. Abi heard her
walking down the corridor.

Flame began calmly washing his face.

'How come Keera didn't see you?'
Abi asked him.

Flame rubbed a paw across his
whiskers. 'Magic. I choose who sees
me,' he explained.

'You mean you can make yourself
invisible? That's going to make things
much easier. It's always really busy in
schools and as there's no pets allowed,
it's probably best if you only show
yourself to me. OK?' Abi grinned at
Flame as he nodded that he understood.

'This is fantastic! It's going to be so much fun, having you here!'

Flame purred back, his eyes narrowing to pleased slits.

Chapter
THREE

The next few days passed by quickly. Abi was kept busy with lessons, making new friends and finding her way around. She and Sasha got on really well. She wished Flame could show himself to Sasha too but, for Flame's safety and the sake of the school rules, the fewer people who knew the better.

Flame came everywhere with her.
During lessons, he curled up on a
nearby window sill or jumped on top
of a bookcase. Abi loved having him
around. He was her special invisible
secret. It was only at night when she
lay in bed that she felt homesick.

Flame snuggled up next to her. Abi
cuddled him and Flame closed his eyes
and purred softly. 'Are you homesick

29

too?' she whispered, stroking his soft fur.

'Miss good friends.' Flame nodded with a sigh.

Abi kissed the top of his head sleepily. It was comforting to hug his warm little body. 'We'll just have to look after each other.'

Abi woke one morning to find Sasha already up and dressed. 'Hurrah! It's Saturday! No lessons. A day to ourselves,' Sasha said grinning. 'What shall we do?'

Abi's hands flew to her face. 'Cripes! I almost forgot. It's netball practice! They're choosing teams today.' She jumped out of bed and began throwing her clothes on.

Flame sat on the window sill. The

morning sun made his black and white coat gleam softly.

'Do you mind if I come?' Sasha asked.

'Course I don't! But I didn't think you liked netball,' Abi said, stuffing her gym kit into her sports bag.

Sasha grinned. 'I don't! I'm rubbish at sports. But I like watching. I can be your number-one fan, if you like!' she joked.

'As if!' Abi laughed and gave her a friendly shove.

Straight after breakfast, Abi and Sasha made their way to the school gym. Flame had decided to come too. He was curled up in Abi's sports bag.

Some other girls from Abi's lessons were in the changing rooms. They called out a greeting to Abi. 'Hi!'

'Hi!' Abi answered with a smile. She changed into her kit. 'Will you be all right?' she whispered to Flame.

'I will be fine. Go and look around,' he mewed softly.

Abi ran on to the court where some girls were already practising their shooting skills. She saw Keera throw the ball straight into the net.

'Good shot,' shouted Marsha.

Sasha, who was standing on the sidelines next to Keera's other friend, Tiwa, gave Abi an enthusiastic wave.

Keera looked smug. 'In case you didn't know, I'm the school's star shooter,' she told Abi.

Miss Green, the sports teacher, blew her whistle. 'Gather together, everyone.

As you probably know, we play High
Five netball. So let's divide up into
squads. I want to see some team play.'

Abi put on a bib with the letters GS,
for goal shooter. She really liked High
Five. It meant she got a chance to play
in all the different positions.

Keera and her friends put on their
bibs. Tiwa said something to Keera,
who gave Abi a sly look.

On the whistle, the centre passed the ball. Abi and her goal attack teammate worked to get the ball into the circle. Abi saw an opening. She spun round, aimed and scored.

'Well played, Abi!' called Sasha.

'Huh! Lucky shot,' shouted Tiwa.

Abi scored twice more. She was breathing hard when the timekeeper called first quarter, but she was eager for the next game. She loved playing with her new schoolfriends.

'Swap positions, everyone!' Miss Green called out.

Abi changed to goalkeeper and on the other team Keera was playing goal attack. She was really good. Abi had to work hard defending against her. Suddenly Keera broke free. She shot at goal. The ball bounced off the net and went over the line.

'Hard luck!' called Tiwa.

Keera's face twisted. She looked down at the floor and clenched her fists.

As Abi went after the ball, she saw Flame come bounding up the gym. He jumped on a pile of gym mats. Rolling over, he lay stretched out on his back, showing his pale tummy.

Abi couldn't help chuckling. Flame seemed to be really enjoying himself.

She came and stood behind the line, ready to throw in the ball.

'Were you laughing at me?' Keera demanded.

'No,' Abi said, puzzled.

Keera scowled. 'You'd better not be. I hardly ever miss a shot at goal.'

As Abi threw the ball, she suddenly realized that Keera had seen her laughing at Flame. She was going to have to be a lot more careful at keeping him secret.

Moments later, Keera caught a low pass from Marsha. Abi was marking her closely. As Keera twisted round, she seemed to slip. Her elbow shot out and jabbed into Abi's ribs.

'Oh!' Winded, Abi doubled up in pain.

'Foul! She did that on purpose!' Sasha yelled, forgetting to be shy. Her long plait swung about as she jumped up and down in protest.

'Abi's pretending! That didn't hurt,' called Tiwa.

Abi held her side, trying to get her breath.

She heard a low growl. From the corner of her eye, she saw Flame's fur sparkle and his whiskers crackle with electricity. A warm tingling flowed down her spine.

'Uh-oh,' breathed Abi. 'Now what?'

Keera aimed the ball at the net, gathered herself to jump, then sprang into the air. She threw the ball. Up it went, higher and higher. 'Oo-er!' she cried as the ball whizzed right up to the roof beams.

Abi watched in amazement as the ball turned slowly in the air and then zoomed downwards. It hit Keera on the head.

'Ow!' cried Keera. Suddenly she started to spin round. She spun faster and faster on the spot, until she was just a blur!

Chapter
* FOUR *

The gym erupted with laughter. Sasha
laughed too, her hands over her mouth.

'Help! I can't stop!' Keera wailed, her
arms waving about and her gym shoes
squeaking as she pirouetted like a skater
on ice.

Miss Green made a sound of
impatience. 'Keera Moore! Must you
always be the centre of attention?'

Abi had got her breath back now.
She bit back a grin. No one else could
see Flame. There he sat beneath the
goalpost, blinking up at Keera. She
edged towards him. 'Flame,' she gently
scolded.

'She hurt you, Abi.' Flame's eyes
glittered mischievously as the silver
sparks made a fizzing noise around
him and died down.

'I'm OK now,' Abi said. 'You can stop
her spinning now.'

Flame hesitated. He pointed a paw at
Keera.

Keera came to a sudden stop and
stood there swaying gently. 'What
happened?' she groaned.

Marsha and Tiwa ran over to help
her. 'Are you all right?'

'Course I am! Get off me!' snapped
Keera, red-faced with embarrassment.

'What a show-off! I bet she feels sick
after all that spinning!' Sasha came over
to Abi.

Miss Green clapped her hands.
'Drama's over! Take a break, everyone.
Gather round. I want to talk to you.'

Abi took a cup of water from the

drinks dispenser and then went and sat near Sasha.

'Every year we pick a team captain,' Miss Green was saying. 'Brockinghurst is hosting a High Five competition at the end of term. So it's especially important that our captain is someone who inspires others to do their best . . .'

Keera looked smug. She shifted about as if ready to get up.

'. . . so I've decided that this year it'll be – Abi West!'

Keera's jaw dropped. 'But – she's only a rotten little first year!'

'Stand up, Abi,' said Miss Green, frowning at Keera. 'I was impressed by the way you played and you kept a cool head under pressure. That's the kind of captain we need.'

'Me?' Abi gasped in surprise as she rose to her feet. She felt herself blush.

'Well done, Abi,' said Miss Green with a warm smile.

Everyone, except Keera and her friends Marsha and Tiwa, clapped and cheered. Sasha shouted loudest of all.

Abi ate her lunch quickly and then hurried to her room.

Once inside, she poured some milk into a saucer. 'There you are. It's a special treat,' she told Flame.

Flame purred with pleasure. He lapped the milk with his little pink tongue. When he finished drinking, he curled up on her bed and closed his eyes. 'I am sleepy now,' he mewed softly.

Abi stroked him. 'You have a nap. I'm going to the library. I'll see you later.' She picked up a folder and tucked it under her arm.

The library was quiet, so Abi had her choice of the computers. She opened her folder and set to work.

Sasha found her there an hour later. 'I've been looking everywhere for you.' She peered over Abi's shoulder. Her dark eyes opened wide. 'Schoolwork? On a Saturday afternoon?'

Abi felt herself get hot. She hesitated, biting her lip. 'I sometimes need to go over things a few times before I understand them properly,' she admitted after a long pause. 'I bet you think I'm stupid, don't you?'

Sasha shook her head. 'Of course I

don't! Everybody learns in different ways. Anyway, so what? You're fantastic at sports. I could help you if you like.'

'Really? That would be great!' Abi beamed at her friend. Sasha was brilliant at lessons.

They went through the lesson notes together. After another twenty minutes, Abi sat back. 'It all makes much more sense now.'

'See, you can do it,' Sasha said with a smile. 'Do you fancy walking into the village? We could spend our pocket money.'

Abi smiled. 'Sounds like fun. I'll just put my folder back in our room. Shall I meet you at the school gate?'

Sasha nodded.

As Abi hurried out of the library, she saw Marsha coming towards her. Marsha glanced at the folder under Abi's arm but said nothing.

When Abi entered her room, Flame sat up and stretched. He made a little sound of greeting.

'Hello, you.' Abi gave him a cuddle. 'Had a good sleep? I'm just going to the village with Sasha. Do you want to come?'

Flame gave an eager mew. Abi opened her bag and he jumped in.

'Comfortable?' she said, shouldering her bag. 'Let's go.'

Sasha was at the gate. She waved as Abi approached.

It was a warm afternoon. Flame stuck his head out of the bag, enjoying the view as Abi and Sasha sauntered down the road. The village was a cluster of cottages grouped near an old stone bridge that spanned the river.

'There's the newsagent's,' Abi said, walking across a green to a large, thatched cottage that stood by itself. As she and Sasha opened the shop door, a bell rang.

Abi felt Flame jump out of her school bag as he went off looking for exciting smells to explore.

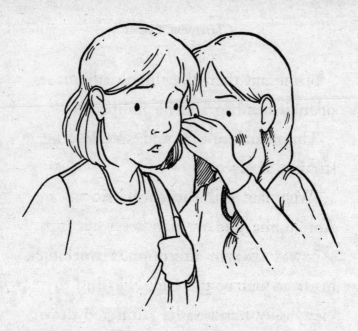

'Oh, no,' Sasha whispered. 'Look who's over there.'

Abi saw Keera flipping through some magazines. Marsha and Tiwa were at the counter buying crisps and drinks.

'Just ignore them. Come on,' Abi said, walking towards a display of sweets. Sasha followed her. She picked up a bag of sherbet lemons. 'My favourites.'

Keera looked up. Abi saw her nudge

Marsha and then the three of them drifted over.

Abi's heart sank, but she looked straight at Keera.

'Well, if it isn't the cheat,' Keera jeered. She put her hands on her hips. 'Marsha saw you doing extra work. You're just trying to get ahead of everybody in class.'

'I'm not!' Abi said. 'I'm just trying to keep up.'

'Oh, yeah, sure!' Tiwa scoffed.

'Leave her alone. She doesn't have to explain herself to you,' Sasha spoke up bravely.

'Who asked you?' Marsha turned on Sasha. 'I shouldn't buy any sweets if I were you. You might get even more spots!'

Keera and Tiwa laughed.

Sasha hung her head. She put a hand up to cover the birthmark on her cheek.

Abi felt her temper rising. She leapt to her friend's defence. 'Leave her alone! She hasn't got spots. It's just a birthmark!'

Marsha jutted her head forward. 'Listen to the cheat sticking up for Spotty. 'Spo-tty! Spo-tty!' she chanted. She knocked the bag of sweets out of Sasha's hands.

'Oh!' Sasha said with dismay as the bag burst. Sweets rolled everywhere.

Abi saw a flash of sparks as Flame leapt on to a nearby shelf. He twitched his whiskers and a fountain of silver sparks shot towards Marsha.

Abi felt her backbone start to prickle. 'Uh-oh . . . now what?' she said under her breath.

There was a horrible squelching noise. First one purple blob appeared on Marsha's cheek, then another. Big blotches began popping out all over Marsha's face!

Chapter
* FIVE *

Keera and Tiwa gaped at Marsha in
horror.

'What's wrong with your face?' Tiwa
said.

'What do you mean?' Marsha went
and peered at herself in the glass
window. Her face was completely
purple and her nose looked all lumpy,
like a blackberry. 'Aargh! What's
happened to me?' she wailed.

'It's probably the Black Death. Stay
away from me!' Keera said.

'Oo-er! It might be catching!' Tiwa
backed away.

Marsha burst into tears.

Abi even felt a bit sorry for her. She
grasped Sasha's arm and hurried
towards the counter. 'Quick! Let's pay
for our sweets and go!'

Marsha had clapped her hands to her

face. Moaning, she stumbled past the counter and tried to open the door with her elbow.

'Are you all right, dear?' The shopkeeper looked at her with concern.

'Mnnnff,' mumbled Marsha, pulling her school sweater over her head.

Keera and Tiwa dashed for the door. Abi saw Keera grab some bags of sweets from the counter while the shopkeeper wasn't looking.

Outside the shop, Abi told Sasha what she had seen. 'Keera stole them! I saw her shove them in her bag!'

'That's awful. Keera gets loads of pocket money. She was bragging about it at lunch. Those three are so mean.' Sasha looked towards Keera and Tiwa who were running down the road.

Marsha was walking more slowly, trying to keep her face covered. 'It's weird what happened to Marsha, isn't it?' She grinned. 'But it serves her right!'

Abi nodded and grinned back. 'Yes! But I bet it won't last long. It's probably just an allergy or something.'

Sasha still looked puzzled. 'Some strange things have been happening at school lately, haven't they?'

'Mmm,' Abi said, looking away.

Suddenly they both heard some shouting. It was coming from near the river. A group of boys were pointing up at a tree. Two of them were nudging each other and laughing. One of them, the biggest, who looked about thirteen, was collecting stones.

'What are they doing?' Abi said.

Sasha shaded her eyes and looked into the tree. 'Oh, no! There's a black and white kitten up there.'

Abi's heart lurched in her chest. It was Flame!

She realized that Flame must have slipped out of the shop and gone exploring. Climbing the tree had been so exciting that he'd forgotten to stay invisible. Now everyone could see him, so he couldn't do any magic to save himself!

Just then Flame slipped. Abi heard him give a yowl of terror as he only just managed to catch on with his paws to a slim branch hanging out over the river. He clung on desperately, his back legs dangling in the air.

'He's going to fall!' Abi gasped.

Leaping forward, she raced towards the boys.

The tough-looking boy had sorted out a stone. He drew his arm back and took aim.

'No!' Abi screamed.

She rushed up and shoved the tough-looking boy hard in the chest. He was so surprised that he backed off in amazement.

Abi stood beneath the branch, arms outstretched over the river. She was only just in time.

Flame gave a howl and fell out of the tree. Abi caught him, hardly noticing as his sharp claws raked her hands and arms.

'I've got you, Flame. You're safe,' she whispered. She cradled his trembling body.

The tough boy had recovered from his surprise and his face darkened with anger. 'Hey, you!' he shouted at Abi.

'Get her, Craig!' one of the other boys called.

Abi realized that Craig was much bigger than her. She glanced at Sasha, who had just reached the tree. 'Run!' she yelled.

Sasha didn't need telling twice. She
and Abi tore off down the road. Flame
nestled against Abi, shivering with
fright.

The boys ran after them.

'Look!' Sasha pointed across a field.
'That's the back of our school. It must
be a short cut!'

Abi spotted a stile. 'Over here!' she
urged.

She and Sasha climbed up and
jumped into the field. Breathing hard,
they pounded across the grass. Abi ran
as fast as she could, but holding Flame
slowed her down. She chanced a look
over her shoulder.

Craig was gaining on her!

Sasha reached the gates. She
dragged them open and raced towards

the school. 'We'll be OK now!'
she called over her shoulder to
Abi.

Abi had one foot inside the gates.
Suddenly she was jerked to a halt.

Craig had grabbed her arm!

Abi struggled to pull free. She
couldn't push Craig away or she might
drop Flame.

Craig's fingers dug into her arm.
'Give me that kitten!' he said through
gritted teeth.

'No!' Abi winced, her heart
pounding. She curled her arms round
Flame and struggled to get away, but
Craig was too strong.

Flame gave a tiny mew and a couple
of silver sparks shot out of his fur. Abi
felt a weak tingle up her spine. Flame

was feeling better and trying to do some magic.

She gathered all her strength and gave a final wrench. Taken by surprise, Craig lost his grip. Abi made a frantic dive inside the gates.

Behind her, Craig gave a yell. 'Help! I'm stuck!'

Abi turned round. Craig's feet seemed rooted to the spot. He waggled his knees, trying to make his legs move. She watched his friends run up and grab his hands. They tried to pull Craig free, but he was stuck fast.

'You big bully!' Abi shouted to Craig as she zoomed down the school path after Sasha. She knew the spell would soon wear off.

Abi didn't look back until she was
inside the building. Half a minute later,
she collapsed against a wall and tried to
catch her breath.

'Gosh! You were brave,' Sasha puffed
beside her. 'That horrible Craig boy
was miles bigger than you!'

Abi didn't feel brave. Now that the
danger was past, her legs felt all weak
and trembling. The scratches on her

hands and arms were stinging like crazy too.

'When did you let that kitten go?' asked Sasha.

'What?' Abi realized that Flame must have made himself invisible. That meant he was feeling back to his old self. 'Oh, he jumped down back there in the field,' she said quickly. 'I bet he lives somewhere close. He'll find his way back. I'm just going up to the room. I want to wash these scratches.'

Sasha decided she was hungry and went off to beg some sandwiches from Cook. 'I'll bring some up to the room for you.'

'OK. Thanks. And could you ask her for some milk, please?' Abi began climbing the stairs.

In her room, Abi sat on her bed with
Flame in her lap. He snuggled up close.
'You saved me, Abi. Thank you. But
are you hurt?' he mewed with concern.

Abi looked at the deep scratches on
her hands. She shrugged. 'It doesn't
matter.'

Flame reached out a paw and
touched her very gently. Tiny silver
sparks, like Christmas glitter, sprinkled
her hands and arms. Abi felt them
grow warm. The pain faded. Where the
scratches had been there were now just
faint marks.

'Thank you, Flame,' she said. 'I nearly
died with fright when I saw you up
that tree!'

She bent her head and Flame
touched her chin with the tip of his

cold black nose. A warm glow settled in Abi's heart. She realized how fond she was of the magic kitten. It made her sad to think that one day he may have to leave.

Chapter
⋆ SIX ⋆

Abi and Sasha were just finishing classes the following day when they were called to Mrs York's office.

Keera, Tiwa and Marsha were already there. Marsha's face had gone back to normal.

Mrs York explained that Mrs Brown from the newsagent's had noticed that some sweets had gone missing. 'She's certain it was just after the five of you left her shop yesterday afternoon. Have you anything to say?' she asked.

'It's nothing to do with me,' Keera said promptly.

Abi's eyes widened. She looked across at Sasha, but by silent agreement neither of them spoke. Abi didn't want to tell tales on anyone, even if it was Keera and her horrible friends. Sasha obviously thought the same way.

Tiwa and Marsha were also silent.

Mrs York looked angry and disappointed. 'I'm going to give the person responsible a chance to own up. You have until tomorrow morning. After that, I shall take steps to find the truth.'

In the corridor outside, Keera
smirked at Abi and Sasha. She went off
with her friends. They heard them
laughing together.

Sasha clenched her fists. 'Ooh!
They make me so mad!' she said. 'I
really feel like going back and telling
the Head that Keera took those
sweets.'

Abi frowned. 'Me too, but I'm not

going to. I hate what Keera did. But I'm not a snitch.'

'But we can't let her get away with it!' Sasha said.

'She won't. My mum says that the truth has a way of getting out,' Abi said. 'Sorry, Sasha, but I've really got to go now. It's netball practice tonight . . .'

'And you've still got that project on Ancient Egyptians to work on, right?' Sasha guessed. 'I was going to computer club, but I can go later. I'll give you a hand.'

'Thanks. You're the best friend anyone could have!' Abi linked arms with Sasha.

By the next morning, no one had owned up to stealing the sweets. Somehow the news had got out and rumours were all over the school.

'I heard that Mrs York is going to do a room search,' Sasha said to Abi when they were sitting eating lunch. 'Maybe Keera will own up before that.'

'I wouldn't hold my breath,' Abi said. 'But I think she might have a guilty conscience.'

'How do you know?' Sasha asked.

'She left netball practice early to go and see Nurse with a headache,' Abi replied.

'Did she?' Sasha looked surprised. 'I saw her and Tiwa outside our room just before you got back. She seemed OK then.'

Just as Abi was finishing her baked potato and salad, she heard someone call her name. 'Mrs York wants to see you,' a girl she had seen round school a few times told her.

Abi rose to her feet. She threw a puzzled glance at Sasha. What could the Head want with her?

'Grounded for a week! But I haven't done anything!' Abi burst out.

She stood in her room, looking with dismay at Mrs York. The head teacher held up three bags of sweets, which she had just found under Abi's bed. 'Then how do you explain these?'

'But they're not mine,' Abi insisted. 'Someone must have put them there.'

Keera! She hid the sweets under my bed, Abi thought. *That's why she left netball practice early!*

'Please. You have to believe me. I

didn't steal those sweets,' Abi said.

Mrs York shook her head. 'I'm sorry you still can't seem to tell me the truth. I expected more of you, Abi. I shall have more to say about this later.' She swept from the room.

Stung by the unfairness of it, Abi sank on to a chair. How was she going to prove her innocence?

'Caught red-handed, were you?' said a gloating voice from the doorway. 'I wouldn't be surprised if they picked someone else to be captain of the netball team now.'

Abi didn't look up. 'Just go away, Keera,' she said in a shaky voice.

Over the next week, Abi tried to throw herself into her schoolwork. But it was no use. She couldn't seem to concentrate.

'Keera's telling everyone that you're the thief. We can't let her get away with this!' Sasha fumed at the end of a maths lesson. 'I've had enough. I'm going to see Mrs York right now!'

Abi put her things back into her pencil case. 'It's too late for that. Mrs

York will just think you're sticking up for me. She'll never believe me after she found the sweets under my bed.'

'If only there was some way to *make* Keera tell the truth,' Sasha said.

An idea suddenly sprang into Abi's mind. She sat up straight. 'That's it! You're brilliant, Sasha!'

'Am I?' Sasha blinked at her.

Abi's idea was taking shape. She grinned. 'Remember that first day, how Keera tried to scare us about the school ghost?'

Sasha nodded. 'The Grey Lady.'

'Exactly!' Abi said. 'I think I might have a way to scare Keera into telling the truth. But I'll need your help.'

'Fine. Just tell me what to do,' Sasha said.

'OK. This is the plan . . .'

When Abi had finished, a slow smile spread over Sasha's face. 'I think I get the idea!

That evening, Abi rolled up her bed sheet, tucked it under her arm and set off with Flame. They made their way along the twists and turns of the old stairways, up to the dusty landing. There were the narrow windows of thick, greenish glass that Abi remembered. In front of her was the ancient wooden door.

As Abi opened it, it seemed to groan in protest. She gave a small shiver. It was even creepier up here than she remembered, especially in the fading light.

She wrapped herself in the sheet.
'OK. Do you remember what to do?'
she asked Flame.

Flame nodded and gave her a
whiskery grin. 'I am ready.'

Abi heard footsteps on the stairs.
'Quick! They're coming!'

She pushed the door so that it almost
closed. Slipping the sheet over her
head, she melted into the shadows.

Little prickles of warmth tickled her
spine. Beside her, Flame began to
crackle and fizz with silver sparks.

'I'm going back. We're completely
lost!' Keera's sulky voice echoed in the
stairwell.

'It's just up here, honest. The room's
full of brilliant sports equipment,' Sasha
said. 'I found it by accident. No one
else knows about it.'

'OK, but you'd better be right about
this,' Keera warned.

'Wait for it,' Abi whispered to Flame.

As Sasha pushed the door wide open,
it gave a loud creak.

'Now!' Abi hissed.

She felt herself rising in the air.
Higher and higher she floated.

'Whoo-oo-oh!' she wailed, flapping

her arms. 'Keera Moore. I know you stole those sweets,' she said in what she hoped was a ghostly voice.

'Aargh!' Keera screamed. 'Leave me alone. I'm sorry I stole them!'

'You must own up to what you did,' Abi said, sounding as spooky as she could.

'All right. Please don't haunt me, Grey Lady!' Keera pleaded.

Abi heard a scuffle and then footsteps running down the stairs. Keera had run away!

'OK, you can let me down,' she whispered to Flame. She drifted down and felt her feet touch the ground. Throwing off the sheet, she gave Flame a quick cuddle. 'That was great! Thanks, Flame.'

Flame mewed softly. 'You are welcome.'

Sasha was waiting on the landing when Abi stepped out of the dark room. She grinned broadly. 'You were brilliant! I wish you could have seen Keera's face! I thought she was going to faint with fright! Even I was scared. It looked like you really were floating.'

'It must have been a trick of the light,' Abi improvised. 'Bet you a week's pocket money that Keera's on her way to see Mrs York right now!'

Chapter
* SEVEN *

Abi and Sasha had a break before the next lesson. They had taken some drink and crisps into the school grounds. It was a warm day and they sat on the grass.

'I can't believe the Head let Keera stay in the netball team,' Sasha said. 'And she only got grounded for a couple of days! Just because she put on a big act and went and said sorry to Mrs Brown at the newsagent's.'

'I know. It doesn't seem fair, does it? I hate to admit it, but we'd really miss having Keera in the team. She's a really good player,' Abi said. 'Anyway, I'm just pleased that my name's cleared.'

'Me too. How's netball going?' Sasha asked.

'Really good. Miss Green's a great teacher. She makes you want to do your best,' Abi enthused. 'She says the team's starting to play together as a unit. And she thinks we've got a chance of beating the other schools in the tournament.'

'That's great,' Sasha said. 'It's not that far away, is it?'

Abi shook her head. 'No. I can't
believe we're halfway through term. It's
gone so quickly.'

Sasha leaned back on her elbows,
enjoying the sunshine. She watched
Keera, Marsha and Tiwa walk past in
the distance.

Abi glanced at Flame. He was chasing
a butterfly, batting at it with his front
paws. It fluttered away and he rolled

over and began biting his tail. She chuckled, feeling a surge of affection for him.

'What are you laughing at?' asked Sasha.

'Oh, nothing,' Abi replied.

Sometimes, she forgot that no one else could see Flame. But she never forgot how important it was to keep him a secret. Somewhere out there, fierce cats from Flame's own world were searching for him. And if they ever found him, they would kill him.

The next few weeks passed quickly. Abi hardly had time to think. She concentrated on keeping up with her schoolwork and fitting in netball practice in any spare moments, and then, one morning, she woke with a sinking feeling.

'We get our results for our schoolwork today,' she whispered to Flame while Sasha was in the shower. 'I just know I'm going to get rotten marks.'

Flame licked her hand with his rough little tongue. 'But you have worked hard,' he sympathized.

'I know. I've done loads of extra study. But I'm not sure it'll be enough.'

Flame looked up at her with big round eyes. 'I can fix this for you,' he mewed helpfully.

Abi shook her head. She tickled his ears. 'No. That would be cheating. Thanks, anyway, Flame. But I have to face up to this one myself.' She flung back the duvet and jumped out of

bed. 'Come on. Let's go outside for a
walk. There's plenty of time before
breakfast.'

Flame jumped down eagerly.

Sunshine streamed into the room as
Abi flung on her school clothes and
dragged a brush through her hair. Once
outside, she and Flame crossed the
playing field and went towards a small
wood.

Flame tore about the woodland floor, his ears laid flat to his head. He chased wind-blown leaves and snuffled up all the exciting smells in the grass.

Abi relaxed as she smiled at his antics. He loved exploring outside.

She had a sudden thought. 'Do you have trees and grass where you come from?'

'Yes. And rivers. And mountains. But no people. Just my kind,' Flame told her.

A world with only cats, Abi thought, *how strange that must be*. She would love to see it.

Flame seemed to know what she was thinking. 'Magic will take me back to my world one day. I do not know when but I do know it will only be strong enough for one,' he said sadly.

Abi felt disappointed, but she forced a
smile. 'Never mind. I don't suppose
there would be much to eat. I bet you
don't have shops!' she joked.

Flame gave her a whiskery grin. 'We
do not need shops for juicy prey!'

A piece of silvery paper blew towards
Abi. She picked it up and screwed it
into a ball and then threw it across the
grass. Flame scampered after it. He

rolled over and over, scrabbling at the paper ball with his front and back paws.

Abi laughed fondly. It was so perfect having Flame here. She didn't want anything to ever change.

Chapter
EIGHT

'Abi, come and look. It's our results!'
Sasha called Abi over to the
noticeboard outside the classroom.
They had just finished a maths lesson.

'What's it say?' Abi hardly dared
look.

'You're tenth out of the whole class.
And you got top marks for your
Ancient Egypt project,' Sasha read.

'Really? That's fantastic!' Abi's spirits soared. She felt like she could jump to the moon.

'You deserve it,' Sasha said generously.

'Thanks,' Abi said. 'But I couldn't have done it without your help. Wow! Look at your marks. You're second in the class. I bet your mum and dad will be dead proud.'

Sasha blushed, but she smiled. 'I expect they will. I'm really looking forward to seeing them for the holidays.'

Abi nodded. 'School's great, isn't it? But I miss my mum and dad too.'

'You'll see them in a few days, won't you? At the netball tournament?' Sasha reminded her.

'Oh, yes. They're coming to watch. It's going to be great. I'm on my way to practice now. There's only a couple left.'

Sasha walked part of the way with her. She stopped by an open classroom with rows of computers. Sasha was helping to design and produce the programmes for the tournament.

'See you later,' Sasha said. 'Have a good practice.'

In the gym, Miss Green chose squads for a practice match. Abi played in goal attack position and Keera was goal shooter. They worked well together on the court, feeding each other to score goals.

'Well played, you two,' Miss Green said. 'Keep up the good work.'

Abi and Keera made their way in silence to the showers afterwards. Abi had enjoyed the game. 'You're a really good player, Keera,' she said a bit reluctantly.

Keera looked surprised. 'Thanks,' she said. There was a long pause and then she said quietly, 'You're not bad yourself.'

Abi blinked at her. Keera was being almost human! Maybe she really had learned her lesson and decided to change. Wait until she told Sasha!

When Abi got back to their room, Sasha was already there.

'How was computer club?' Abi asked brightly.

'Oh . . . er, it was OK, thanks.' Sasha

had her head down. She reached across to the bedside table for a tissue and blew her nose.

Abi could tell she had been crying. 'What's wrong?'

'I've just had a phone call from my mum and dad.' Sasha gulped back tears. 'They won't be coming home. They have an important business deal to do or something. So I have to stay at school over the holidays.'

'Oh, no. What a shame!' Abi sat down next to Sasha and put her arm round her shoulder. 'Maybe it won't be so bad. I bet there'll be other girls staying here too.'

Sasha nodded miserably. 'I know. But it won't be the same as going home, will it?'

Abi had to agree that it wouldn't.
She would hate to have to stay at
school when term ended. Poor
Sasha.

While she finished eating supper, Abi
thought about how she could cheer
Sasha up.

The dining room was full of laughter
and chatting voices. But Sasha took no
notice. She pushed her food around on

her plate. It was chocolate pudding, her favourite, but she had eaten only a spoonful.

'Do you want to walk to the village?' Abi suggested.

Sasha shook her head. 'I don't really feel like it.'

Abi tried again. She reached into her school bag. 'I've got a brilliant new wildlife magazine. You can read it first, if you like.'

Sasha shrugged, but then she took the magazine. 'OK. Thanks.'

'I'm worried about Sasha,' Abi said later to Flame. 'I really want to make her feel better, but I don't know what to do.'

Flame rubbed his head against her

chin, making little comforting noises.
'Sasha is sad. Magic cannot help her,' he
mewed.

'No,' Abi agreed, stroking him gently.
'I don't suppose it can.'

She frowned, thinking hard. There had
to be something she could do. Suddenly
an idea came to her. 'I've got it! I know
what to do to cheer her up!'

Chapter
* NINE *

When Abi woke the next day, she was keen to put her plan into action. She would have to speak to her mum and dad about it first, but today was the day of the tournament and they would be here soon. She couldn't wait.

Abi looked out of the window as the first coaches arrived. A banner hung

over the car park entrance. It read:
'Welcome to Brockinghurst School
Tournament.'

Abi felt really excited. The previous
afternoon, the whole school had worked
together on getting ready for the festival.
She had helped set out chairs in the gym
and pin up notices. Sasha had put
programmes on all the chairs.

Even Keera, Marsha and Tiwa did
their share.

'Those three seem really different,'
Sasha commented.

'Yes,' Abi agreed. She would have
loved to explain how Flame had
secretly helped her and Sasha to teach
them a lesson!

'Shall we go down? I'm helping with
welcoming and signing in,' Sasha said.

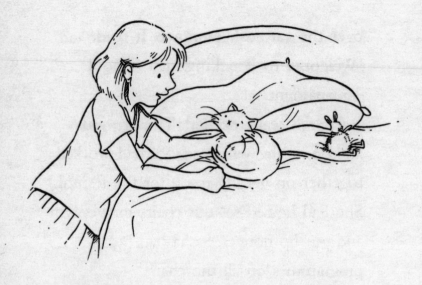

'I'll come down in a minute,' Abi
said. When Sasha had gone, she turned
to Flame. 'Are you coming to watch
the match?' she asked eagerly.

Flame was on her pillow. He had
curled up into a tight ball. 'I will stay
here,' he decided.

'Really? Won't you be bored?' Abi
looked at Flame in astonishment.
Usually he loved to be where any

action was. She bent down and stroked the top of his head. 'I have to go. I promised to help Miss Green set out the cones and stuff for the warm-up.'

Flame raised his head. His eyes seemed troubled. 'Be well, Abi. Be strong,' he mewed softly.

'I will be. I'm fine,' Abi said. 'Don't worry about me.'

She gave him a quick cuddle before leaving the room. He seemed in a strange mood.

Just as Abi reached the gym she spotted two familiar figures. They waved at her. 'Abi, darling!'

'Mum! Dad!' she cried, flinging herself at them for a hug. 'It's so good to see you. I have to ask you something. It's about Sasha . . .'

'Whoa there! Slow down, Abi,' Mr West said with a grin. 'Start again from the beginning.'

Abi took a deep breath and explained her idea to her mum and dad. She crossed her fingers, waiting nervously for their response.

They both smiled.

'Sounds fine to me,' said Mrs West. She glanced at her husband. 'What about you?'

'I think it's a wonderful idea!' Mr West ruffled Abi's hair.

'Yes!' Abi did a little dance of joy. 'Fantastic. Sorry. Got to go and get changed. See you later!'

Abi put on her gym kit. She was setting out cones on the courts when she spotted Sasha near the team benches.

'Sasha!' she called, hurrying over. 'I've got something to tell you. You're not staying here for the school holidays.'

Sasha looked surprised. 'I'm not?'

'No. You're coming home to stay with me. I asked Mum and Dad and they think it's a great idea. What do you think?'

A big grin spread over Sasha's face. Her dark eyes shone. 'That's brilliant! I'd love to come. Thanks, Abi.'

'I can't wait. We're going to have a fantastic time!' Abi gave Sasha a hug.

Just then a voice came through the loudspeaker. It was time for the tournament to begin.

Chapter
* TEN *

As Abi fastened her bib and looked
round at Keera and her other teammates,
the excitement built inside her.

'Round one,' the loudspeaker
announced.

As captain, Abi led her squad to the
players' benches. She sat watching as
the other schools' squads played. Then
it was time for their game.

'Let's play ball!' Abi gave the players high fives.

'Good luck, Abi!' Sasha called from the crowd.

Abi's squad played well. They won their first match by fifteen goals to ten.

'We're through to the next round! Well done, girls,' Miss Green praised.

Their next match was more

challenging. The squad scraped through by only eighteen goals to seventeen.

The following rounds were tough, but to Abi's and everyone's delight they managed to win every game that came their way.

Abi flopped on to the team bench, red-faced and sweaty. She gulped a drink as she watched the play-off for third and fourth places.

Finally the loudspeaker rang out. 'And now, the finals for this year's inter-school tournament.'

Keera stood up. She looked across at Abi. 'We can win this,' she said.

Abi grinned. 'Let's do it!'

As Abi's squad ran on to the court, the school cheered and waved. 'Come on, Brockinghurst!'

Abi played for all she was worth. She scored four goals and Keera scored five. It was the last minute of the game. Abi jumped high at a catch, but she landed awkwardly and her foot went over the sideline.

The umpire blew her whistle. 'Penalty!'

The other squad took the throw-in. They scored a goal. It was now fourteen goals each.

Abi felt furious with herself. What a stupid mistake.

'Hard luck,' Keera said generously.

Abi threw Keera a grateful smile, but they still needed to score again to win and there were only minutes left to play.

The players regrouped. Abi caught the ball and passed to Keera.

Keera spun round and aimed, but it was a difficult angle. There was only one chance to score. Would she be able to do it?

Abi had a better shot. 'To me, Keera!' she called.

Keera looked round.

Abi held her breath. Would Keera give away her chance of a winning goal?

With only seconds to go before the whistle, Keera passed to her. Abi aimed. She scored!

The umpire blew the whistle. Abi's team had won the tournament!

Cheering broke out in the gym. 'Abi! Abi!' Abi's classmates chanted her name.

'Well played, Abi,' Keera said.

Abi smiled. 'You gave me the chance of the winning goal,' she said. She took hold of Keera's hand and held it up. 'We did it together.'

'Abi! Keera!' rang out the cheers.

Keera's cheeks went pink. She gave Abi a hug. Abi returned it, her face glowing. 'Friends?' she said.

Keera beamed at Abi. 'Don't push it!' she joked.

★

Abi lined up with Keera and the rest of the squads and Mrs York presented the certificates. Afterwards, there was a special tea on the lawn.

Abi showed her certificate to her parents.

'Well done,' Mrs West said delightedly. 'And you're doing so well in class. You seemed to have settled in here really well.'

'I wasn't sure I would at first,' Abi said. She turned and linked arms with Sasha. 'But now I love it here. And I've made some great friends.'

Sasha blushed. She grinned from ear to ear.

Suddenly amid all the celebrations, Abi felt uneasy. Something cold prickled up her spine.

She gasped.

Flame! He must be in danger.

She realized now why he had been acting strangely. She knew she had to get to Flame as soon as she could.

'I . . . I have to do something. I'll be right back!' Abi blurted out an excuse to her parents, already racing for a side door.

Somehow she knew just where Flame would be. She wove through the narrow corridors until she came to the staircase. Dashing up the stairs two at a time, she reached the landing. The dusty old door to the storeroom was wide open.

'Flame? Where are you? Are you OK?' Her eyes searched the darkness, looking for the fluffy black and white kitten.

'Abi?' came a deep velvety rumble from the shadows.

A large white lion with glowing white fur stepped forward. He smiled, showing long, sharp teeth.

'Prince Flame!' Abi's breath caught in her throat. She had almost forgotten how startling he was in his true form. 'You're . . . leaving?' she stammered.

Flame nodded. 'Cirrus has come to help me.'

Now Abi noticed another older-looking lion. He was grey and had a kind, wise face.

'I must go now. Uncle Ebony's spies are very close,' Flame growled.

Abi dashed forward. She clung on to
Flame and buried her face in his silky
white fur. 'Take care,' she whispered.
She forced herself to let him go and
backed away.

Flame's fierce emerald eyes crinkled
in a smile. 'Abi, you are a good friend.
Farewell. I will not forget you.'

Silver sparks whirled in the air
around the two lions. The sparks spun

faster and faster, like a tornado. Flame raised a paw in a final wave. His claws glittered like crystal and then he and the older lion were gone.

Abi stared at the empty space, her heart aching.

She would miss Flame horribly, but he was safe and that was the most important thing. It had been brilliant to share her first term with the magic kitten. She would never forget all the fun they'd had. It would remain her secret, forever.

Her eyes pricked with tears, but she blinked them away. She had the holidays with Sasha to look forward to. Smiling at the thought, Abi turned and ran down the stairs.

A Summer Spell

Flame needs to find a purrfect new friend!

And that's how Lisa's boring summer is transformed when a tiny marmalade kitten comes into her life . . .

puffin.co.uk

Star Dreams

Flame needs to find a purrfect new friend!

And that's how Jemma's biggest dreams become possible when a silky cream and brown kitten comes into her life ...

puffin.co.uk

Magic Kitten

Double Trouble

Flame needs to find a purrfect new friend!

And that's how Kim manages
to put up with her mean
cousin when a fluffy silver
tabby kitten comes to stay...

Win a Magic Kitten goody bag!

An urgent and secret message has been left for Flame
from his own world, where his evil uncle is
still hunting for him.

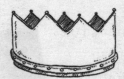

One word from the message can be found in a royal lion
crown hidden in each of the Magic Kitten books 1–4.
Find the hidden words and put them together to complete
the message. Send it in to us and each month we will
put every correct message in a draw and pick out one lucky
winner who will receive a purrfect Magic Kitten gift!

Send your secret message, name and address on a postcard to:
Magic Kitten Competition
Puffin Books
80 Strand
London WC2R 0RL

Hurry, Flame needs your help!

Good luck!

puffin.co.uk

Visit:
penguin.co.uk/static/cs/uk/0/competition/terms.html
for full terms and conditions

Magic Kitten

A Summer Spell
0–141–32014–1

Classroom Chaos
0–141–32015–X

Star Dreams
0–141–32016–8

Double Trouble
0–141–32017–6

puffin.co.uk

Coming Soon . . .

Moonlight Mischief
0–141–32153–9

A Circus Wish
0–141–32154–7

puffin.co.uk